Best Wishes,
Bill & Sally
Fletcher

The Universe Is My Home

✳ A Children's Adventure Story ✳

Story and Pictures by

Bill and Sally Fletcher

Science & Art Publishing
Malibu, CA

It was still dark when Sarah heard the knock on her bedroom door. "Wake up," she heard her dad whisper, "it's time to get ready."

"OK, Dad," she said as she rubbed the sleep from her eyes.

Sarah and her dad were excited about their weekend trip to the desert and were getting started before sunrise. They had just bought a new telescope and this was their first chance to get away from the bright lights of the city to look through it.

They dressed, ate breakfast, and soon were on their way to pick up Sarah's cousin, Robert. This was Robert's first trip to the desert.

When they got there, they set up their camp. By sunset, they had the telescope ready.

"I love the twilight," Sarah said to Robert. "Watch how the stars get brighter and brighter, as the sky gets darker and darker."

"I've never seen so many stars," Robert said.

"Do you see that big long cloud?" Sarah asked. "That's not a normal cloud. It is actually millions of stars that are so far away their light blends together. It's called the Milky Way."

They stayed up past midnight looking through the telescope. They looked at the Moon and at the planet Saturn with its beautiful rings. They looked at star clusters, which are groups of stars that are close together. They even saw an odd-shaped cloud of gas and dust called a nebula.

"Dad," Sarah said looking up from the telescope, "I wonder if there is someone out there on another planet with a telescope looking back at us."

He laughed, but then thought about it for a moment. "Well, there are lots of stars out there similar to our sun. I guess any one of them could have formed with planets where there could be life."

She turned back to the telescope and said softly, "I wish I could meet them, if they are out there. I really do."

By now everyone was tired from the long and exciting day. They got into their sleeping bags and looked up at the starry sky until they drifted off to sleep.

Suddenly Sarah woke up. A strange, almost musical, whistling sound was coming from the rocks near their camp. She looked toward her dad, but he was still asleep.

Slowly, she crept over to the rocks and saw a soft glowing light coming from within them.

Something about the light made her unafraid, so she walked around the rocks to see what was there.

"Oh," she gasped. She had found a most unusual thing.

There were two round bubbles. One was large, a little bigger than she was. The other was quite small and glowed with a yellow light.

She walked around the large bubble wondering what it could be. When she reached out to touch it, a voice said, "Hello, Sarah."

She turned toward the small yellow bubble where the voice had come from. "Hello, Sarah," she heard again. "My name is Andra."

Sarah felt such a thrill. This was the friendliest voice she had ever heard, and she instantly knew that Andra was her friend.

"I heard your wish," Andra said. "I was on my planet looking out at the stars when you wished that you could meet me."

Sarah hesitated. This was a very odd moment!

"Would you like to come with me to see my planet?" Andra asked. "We can be back by morning before your dad wakes up. You can travel in the big bubble."

Sarah's face lit up with a smile.

Just then she felt a hand on her shoulder and turned around to see Robert standing behind her. "I've been listening to everything," he said. "I want to go, too!"

"Of course," Andra said to Robert. "There's plenty of room."

"But how do we get in the bubble?" he asked.

"Just close your eyes and picture yourself inside. You'll see. . . it's easy!"

Sarah held Robert's hand as they closed their eyes and imagined themselves inside. They thought nothing had happened, but when they opened their eyes, they were inside the bubble sailing up and away from the Earth. Andra was right outside their bubble as they flew out into space.

"Look how beautiful the Earth is!" Sarah exclaimed.

Soon they were far away from the Earth and could see several other planets.

There was Jupiter with its red belts of gas—the yellow, ringed planet Saturn—the huge blue-green planet Neptune—and Earth.

"There are nine planets that circle our Sun," Sarah told Robert, "and most of them have moons. Together they make up what is called our solar system."

"You have a beautiful solar system," Andra said, "and you live on a beautiful planet. All of the Universe we are going to see is your home, too, if you choose to think of it that way."

Leaving the solar system far behind them, they traveled through the stars. They had no sensation of speed, yet Sarah knew that something very unusual was allowing them to travel the distances of the stars so quickly. Up ahead they saw a bright pink cloud. "What's that?" Sarah asked.

"That's the great Orion Nebula," answered Andra. "A nebula is a place where gases and dust have collected in space."

"It's so big," Robert said. "Bigger than thousands of stars."

"Yes," Andra answered. "In fact, this is a star nursery. New stars are being born right now out of the gas and dust of this nebula!"

"What's over there with all the different colors?" Robert asked. "Can we go see that?"

Quickly the bubble turned and headed toward it. "I know this one," Sarah said. "I've seen pictures of it. It's called the Horsehead Nebula."

Andra said, "Let's fly through all the colors!" As the bubble raced toward the blue part, they could see the gas and dust of the nebula reflecting the light of a bright blue star.

Then they turned and went past the dark horsehead and plunged into the red glowing cloud. This was great fun!

As quickly as they had come to it, the nebula was now far behind them.

"There's something very special I want to show you," Andra said. "All of the stars you have seen are part of a group of billions of stars that stay together like an island in space. This huge group of stars is called a galaxy—the Milky Way Galaxy.

"If you look over there, far past the stars of our Milky Way Galaxy, you can see another huge island of stars. That one is called the Whirlpool Galaxy. It is the home of a hundred billion more stars."

Their bubble moved closer and closer to a bright yellow star. "That looks like our sun," Robert said.

"Yes it does," Andra replied, "but this is my sun, and my planet is just around the other side."

They approached the planet and stopped above it. "I live down under that big white cloud."

"Oh, please, can we go down and see it closer?" Sarah asked.

With Andra in the lead, they went down toward the surface of the planet.

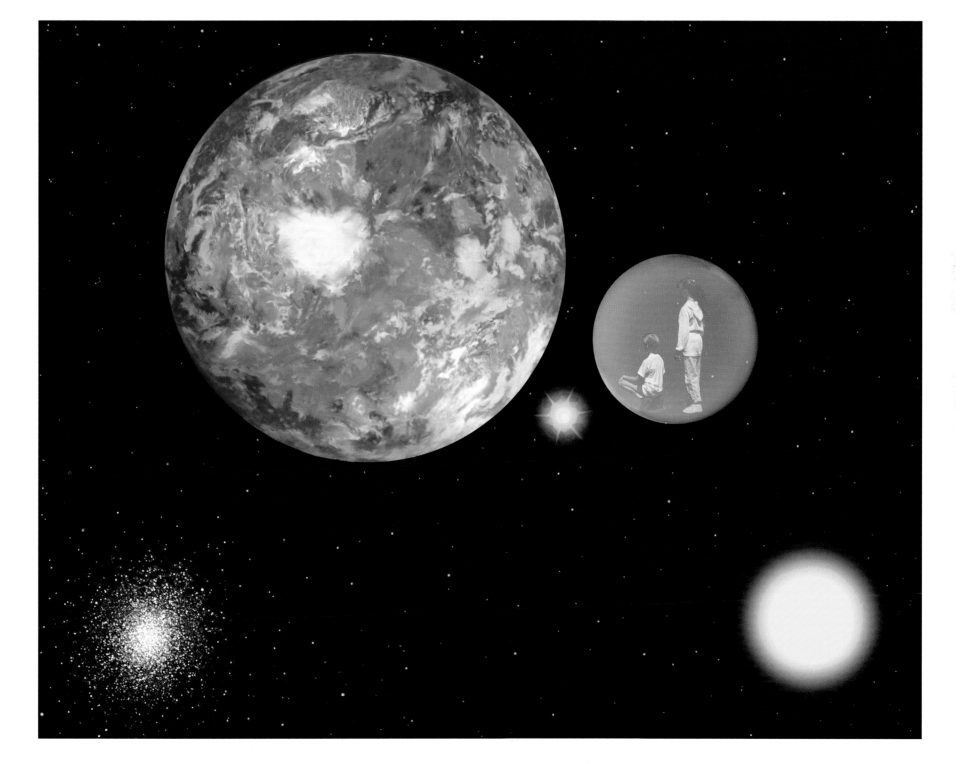

When they sailed under the big white cloud, Sarah and Robert could not believe their eyes. They saw thousands of glowing yellow bubbles lined up in two rows over a colorful valley.

"They've all come to greet you," Andra said as they began to pass in between the rows. Each yellow bubble lit up a little brighter as they passed by.

When they reached the end of the rows, they flew up and over a forest of trees so tall, they grew up through the clouds.

They climbed higher and higher over a blue mountain, until finally they were back in space looking down on the planet.

"We just barely have enough time to get back to your planet before sunrise," Andra said.

"I'm so glad you came to meet us," said Sarah. "Do you think we can meet again someday?"

The yellow bubble moved closer to Sarah. "Just remember how strong your wishes can be. The more you feel them in your heart, the farther they go. Maybe you'll even discover a way to come to me!"

As they moved away from the planet and past the giant star cluster, Sarah and Robert were too tired to stay awake any longer. They both lay down in the bubble and fell fast asleep.

"Wake up, Sarah. I've made breakfast for you and Robert."

Sarah opened her eyes and saw her dad kneeling next to her. "You must have been very tired," he said. "You never sleep this late."

Everything about the night before she remembered perfectly. It wasn't a dream, she was sure—it felt too real to her. But she wondered if anyone was going to believe her.

Just then Robert woke up and sat straight up in his sleeping bag. His eyes were as big as two moons, and his smile stretched from ear to ear.

"Oh, Sarah," he said. "Wait until I tell you about the dream I had last night!"

To Kanchan and her parents

Published by Science & Art Publishing
P.O. Box 1166   Malibu, CA 90265

Library of Congress Catalog Card Number: 92-62242

ISBN 0-9634622-0-2

Printed in the United States of America

10 9 8 7 6 5 4 3 2 1

✳ *All photographs, through-the-telescope astrophotos and computer graphic images are by the authors
with the exception of the planetary images of Jupiter, Saturn, Neptune and Earth which are NASA photos.* ✳

- Our thanks to Breanne and Jerry Fletcher for posing as Sarah and Robert
- Color separating from computer image data by Digital Imaging of Southern California
- Printing and Binding by Horowitz/Rae - Fairfield, NJ